Narky Sharky

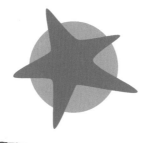

Maverick
Early Readers

'Narky Sharky'
An original concept by Lou Treleaven
© Lou Treleaven

Illustrated by Angelika Scudamore

Published by MAVERICK ARTS PUBLISHING LTD

Studio 11, City Business Centre, 6 Brighton Road,

Horsham, West Sussex, RH13 5BB

© Maverick Arts Publishing Limited August 2020

+44 (0)1403 256941

A CIP catalogue record for this book is available at the British Library.

ISBN 978-1-84886-686-7

www.maverickbooks.co.uk

Green

This book is rated as: Green Band (Guided Reading)
This story is mostly decodable at Letters and Sounds Phase 5.
Up to five non-decodable story words are included.

Narky Sharky

by Lou Treleaven

illustrated by
Angelika Scudamore

Narky Sharky was very narky.

She was grumpy. She was snappy.

Everyone was scared of Narky Sharky,
even her friends.

"Good morning, Narky Sharky," said Friendly Flatfish.

"What's good about it? Nothing! Go away," said Narky Sharky.

"Good morning, Narky Sharky,"
said Jolly Jellyfish.

"It's not a good morning, it's a bad
morning!" said Narky Sharky.
"Goodbye!"

"Good morning, Narky Sharky,"
said Cool Clam. "Chill out, dude."

"And you can shut your shell too," said Narky Sharky.

Her friends tried everything they could to cheer Narky Sharky up.

They hung seaweed round her cave.

They changed the bulb in her anglerfish.

They even polished her
spare rows of teeth.
At least, they tried.

That evening, Narky Sharky

seemed a bit happier.

Her friends crossed their fins.

But in the morning Narky Sharky

was as narky as ever.

Narky Sharky's friends had a secret meeting.

"She's only really scary in the mornings," said Friendly Flatfish.

"Maybe she just hates mornings?"
said Jolly Jellyfish.

"You could be right, man,"
said Cool Clam.

The next morning,

everyone was very quiet.

Friendly Flatfish swam around

extra slowly.

Cool Clam closed his shell
extra quietly.

Jolly Jellyfish stung people extra softly.

And Narky Sharky had a lie in!

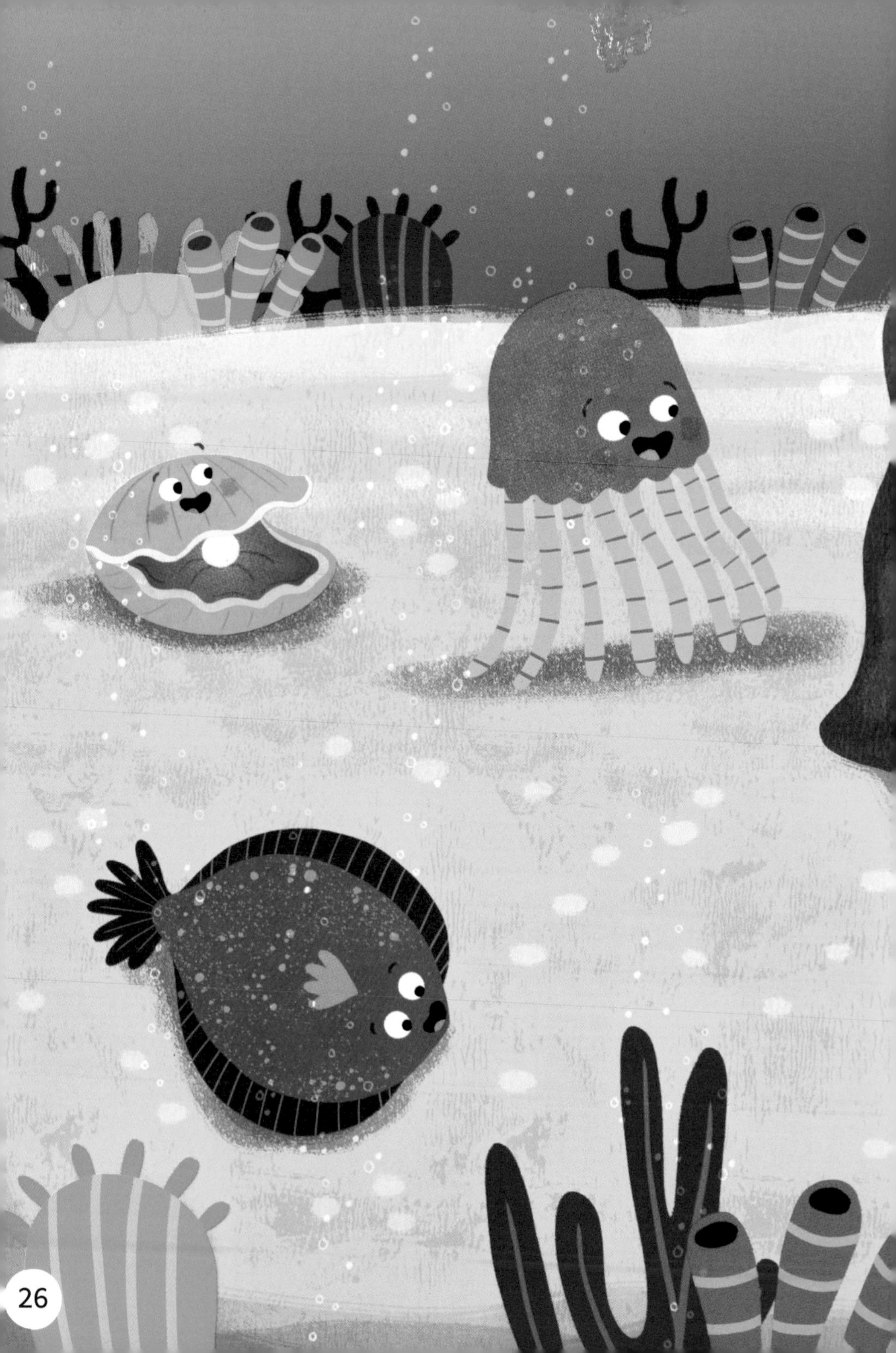

When she finally came out of her cave, Narky Sharky felt much better.

27

And her friends never had to say 'good morning, Narky Sharky' ever again.

They said 'good afternoon,
Sharky' instead!

Quiz

1. What is one of the things Narky Sharky's friends did to cheer her up?
a) Changed the bulb in her anglerfish
b) Threw her a party
c) Made her a cake

2. When is Narky Sharky mostly scary?
a) Mornings
b) Afternoons
c) Evenings

3. What did the friends do to help?
a) They made lots of noise
b) They gave her gifts
c) They were very quiet

4. Narky Sharky had a...
a) Bath
b) Lie in
c) Holiday

5. What do the friends now say to Narky Sharky when she gets up?
a) Hello, Narky Sharky
b) Good afternoon, Sharky
c) Good evening, Shark

Turn over for answers

Book Bands for Guided Reading

The Institute of Education book banding system is a scale of colours that reflects the various levels of reading difficulty. The bands are assigned by taking into account the content, the language style, the layout and phonics. Word, phrase and sentence level work is also taken into consideration.

Maverick Early Readers are a bright, attractive range of books covering the pink to white bands. All of these books have been book banded for guided reading to the industry standard and edited by a leading educational consultant.

Pink
Red
Yellow
Blue
Green
Orange
Turquoise
Purple
Gold
White

To view the whole Maverick Readers scheme, visit our website at
www.maverickearlyreaders.com

Or scan the QR code above to view our scheme instantly!

Quiz Answers: 1a, 2a, 3c, 4b, 5b